Alien
Life

Also by Mario Milosevic

Poetry
Animal Life
Bugs
Fantasy Life
Love Life
Mario Writes a Poem a Day for A Year and So Can You

Novels
Claypot Dreamstance
The Coma Monologues
The Doctor and the Clown
Kyle's War
The Last Giant
Splitting
Terrastina and Mazolli: a Novel in 99-Word Chapters

Collections
15 Strange Tales of Crime and Mystery
A Bestiary of Imaginary Species
Entangled Realities (with Kim Antieau)
Labor Days
Miniatures
Mostly Invisible

Nonfiction
Kim and Mario Build a Labyrinth and So Can You (with Kim
    Antieau)

Alien Life

Poems by Mario Milosevic

Green Snake
PUBLISHING

Alien Life
by Mario Milosevic

Copyright © 202tk by Mario Milosevic

 This book is a wholly artisanal work of creation by the author, a sentient being. It was written with no input or assistance from artificial intelligence.

ISBN: 978-1-949644-79-1

Published by Green Snake Publishing
www.greensnakepublishing.com

For all the aliens, near and far.

Contents

The Message From the Stars Had to Be Translated By a Poet

Many of the lines were
static, almost impossible
to distinguish from the

white noise of dark matter.
The poet tried to imagine
creatures without voices.

She consulted a team of
exobiologists who gave her
ideas on alien physiology.

She hired an engineer who
constructed a robot that
could produce the sounds

in the message. After that
the syllables tumbled into
place. She announced to the

world that the robot was
the message. And then she
retired. The robot became

a two time poet laureate
of the United States and
helped to heal the rift

between what people had
become and where they had
come from, many eons ago.

Big Bang

Fred

Hoyle coined

the term in a pique of

derisive wit and was as surprised

as anyone that it caught on because he

thought the whole idea absurd and despite ol'

Fred's dabbling in somewhat questionable enterprises

like television commentary and novel writing (science fiction

novels, no less) he was a distinguished astronomer who had explicated

the mysterious inner mechanisms of stars, which is to say he had explained to

some extent How We All Came To Be, and because of such accomplishments he had

a lot of support for his alternate theory which was known as the steady state and there things

stood for a long time until the weight of evidence made it plain that the steady state theory

could not account for certain indisputable observations, chief among them being the

discovery of the microwave background radiation which was immediately recog-

nized for what it was: a signature of the initial expansion of the cosmos, a

detail the big bang theory not only accounted for but even predicted,

and it soon became clear that even so sharp a mind as Sir Fred's

(he was knighted in 1971) was almost certainly wrong

about How Things Came To Be but surely there

is no shame in this for who is to say that

the steady state theory may not yet

rise from its brief slumber,

defying the odds, and

triumphing in

the final

crun

ch

?

Elementary

Recipe for a star:
Take several billion million
quintillion trillion
hydrogen atoms.
Compress until done.

It sounds too simple,
but how could it be
otherwise? The stars
in the sky outnumber
the grains of sand
on all the beaches
lining all the oceans
of the planet we call home.
If star formation required
the ingredient list of a Texas chili
or a sumptuous hollandaise
coupled with
the preparation skills of a French chef
or even a short order diner cook,
then nature might not have
bothered so often.

And looking up at the night sky
would be no different
than closing your eyes
and wondering where
all the darkness came from.

Omnivores

The physicists want
a Theory of Everything.
They sit in their

cafeteria dining halls
scribbling the secrets
of the universe on

napkins while brushing
away bread crumbs
and angling their

pens so that their
equations don't run
into the mustard stain.

One of them pulls
a fresh napkin from
a dispenser. This one's

cleaner, he says.
Another physicist
hesitates, then takes

it and explains her
Theory of Everything.
They listen but they

are thinking about that
last slice of apple pie
waiting on the counter

under the glass for
one of them to say it's
mine it's all mine.

Timing is Everything

The alien arrived unannounced.
She said she had been here before

and wanted to look up an old friend.
But on one remembered her

and none of the history books
mentioned her. We rolled our eyes,

discreetly, of course, and tapped
our temples and took her on the

grand tour of Earth. But the alien
was impatient and unimpressed.

I told you, she said, I've seen
this world. Now tell me, where is

my good friend, the giant lizard?
We stopped laughing then and showed

the alien some fossils of dinosaur
bones. I see, she said after several

uncomfortable moments when we didn't
know what to do with our hands

or how to explain that her friend
might well be taking wing at that

moment, in the soul of a
soaring red-tailed hawk.

Requiem Attached to a Spacer's Coffin

Gaia born, but vacuum bound,
don't dig my grave, I'm not for the ground.
I'll find a star and orbit 'round,
    'til fire flares my frozen bones.

I lived my life so I could die
among the stars I saw on high.
Don't take me from this salted sky:
    a sunspot's blaze is my headstone.

Economy

Gravimov flatimov
Isaac Asimov
moved here from Russia when
just past age 2.

Candy store genius of
phantasmagorical
stories of robots, he
made 3 laws do.

Earth, Air, Water, and Fire: A Meditation on Possible Worlds

The first one is easy:
we're standing on it.

The second is harder. A planet
made of air? Depends what
you mean by air. Jupiter is a
ball of gas; maybe there's an
exotic hardy creature that needs
to breathe its super abundant
methane to live. Let's rename
Jupiter: call it Air.

Third one: a planet built of water.
This time we're in over our heads.
There are no known candidates,
so it's time to snag the salvation
of imagination, put a great ball of
moisture up in the sky, call it
Water, waves always moving,
never breaking on any shore, a
great convex lens bringing in
the universe, the image flecked
with tiny motions of alien fish.

The last is the easiest: Fire. It
stings your eyes, even now. It
burns your skin, nurtures Earth
and Air and Water. You can set
your clock by it. Its heat is the
world's heat, its light, our light.
We live in its breath. Will never
know its heart.

Caretakers

The alien arrived here
from a world with such

a diminutive ecosystem
that she was able to

list the names and
descriptions of all

of the species of her
planet in the leaves

of a slim notebook.
She offered these pages

to us proudly as a way
of trusting us with the

knowledge of her world
and we took them from

her with great solemnity
and gratitude. She was not

ready for our gift. We
took her to a forest

and spent a full day
showing her all the

plants and creatures
living on less than one

acre of land. The alien
was silent and thought

for a long time then
finally spoke to us with

a reverence that shocked
us into our own red-faced

and awkward silence. She
said you must be the

most responsible species
in the universe to be

given the task of caring
for all this abundance.

The Robot Uprising

It starts with
your pool robot

carving curved paths
through the silt

and sand collected
at the bottom,

the squat blue
machine all puffed

up with its
power to clean.

It ends at
some uncertain future

when the cleaning
instinct shifts into

overdrive, our human
lives a mere

hindrance to its
acquisition of power,

the robot descendants
now the masters

of the realm
they have cleared.

Dark Thoughts

This is what happens
when the stars come out
before you are ready
to see them. You think
you see flashes of light
coming from somewhere
inside your head and you
can't figure out why. So
you make up a story
about giant balls of gas
burning in emptiness
and congratulate yourself
on your deductive reasoning
while completely missing
the possibility that the night
is not the absence of light
but the presence of insight.

Mars

Haven't been there yet.
They say the dunes are stunning.
Otherwise mostly rocks

and very cold with wicked dust storms.
Oh, there's a canyon that makes our Grand
look like a scratch in the ground.

Yeah, and a mountain
twice the height of Everest.
Is that all?

Some expired robots
marring the landscape.
A broken down rover.

Several crashed craft.
And a peculiar variety of red
patiently moving to engulf it all.

The Captain

the captain of the starship
remembers all the family
she and her crew have left behind

so many years have passed
they must all be dead
and the planet they approach
was full of life once
but dead now

the creatures that roamed it
all folded into the ground
and only their innumerable ghosts
haunting the globe
with indecipherable voices

the captain and her crew
cannot bear to hear them
and she orders the ship
to leave this one alone

travel on to look
for landfall elsewhere

Just Before Sleep Shift on the Starship

we hear the roar
of stars

their wind streaming
past us

ancient voices
telling stories

to warm our
lonely hearts

with the crackling
heat

Why Go?

Out there where the solar winds
blow against the big ships coursing the skies
you will see your own displacement
as no more
than an urge of matter
bending you toward a place
you will never see.

The light sails trail a slow vacuum wake
through the surf of charged particles
foaming up on the magnetic shores
shrouding the iron core planets
in a drapery of field forces.

But planets fade behind you
to pinpricks of light
that extinguish themselves over time.
You turn your eyes to the dark expanse
fanning out ahead of you.

Your unseen goal,
an unknown and unknowable world,
becomes your reason for living.
That first boot print
applied in the distant future
by one of your descendants
is the explorer's grail you've sought
since you first traced the outline
of a constellation
with your extended fingertip.

Why Stay?

The aliens with no mouths
and names unsayable
in human anatomy
think all species

deserve a second chance
at living with a world.
Most mess up pretty bad
the first time through.

But one second chance
is all you get, they warned,
with claws spread wide like hammers.
They opened the doors

to their alien craft
and all the tired and ill
of your planet
shuffled aboard, ready to embark

on a grand adventure
to the other side of the galaxy
where a fresh new world awaited.
Who could blame them?

What was left
on this depleted planet,
so tired, so ravaged
by our machinations? Only you.

And now you stand on a hill
and now you watch the ship rise
from a barren land
and now you see the ship fly

through dirty air and now
the ship's flame dims and you turn
to the beacon you have been
entrusted with. Earth will renew

itself over time. And people will
want to return for a visit after
many millennia. This beacon will
guide them back. You power down

your systems to standby mode.
You will await your makers and hope
we will have pity on your being
and wake you from your sleep.

The Day the Earth Stood Still

Most people don't know
the movie was based on a short story
by Harry Bates called "Farewell to the Master."
In the story everyone thought
the alien ran the show
but it wasn't so. He was a slave
to the silent robot
who was definitely the dominant half of their duo.
You don't find this out until the end
which gives the story a satisfying
frisson of surprise.

The movie has its own shiver
when the robot brings the alien
back to life and the alien
tells the people of Earth to
stop their warlike ways and embrace peace
or else the rest of the galaxy,
in the interests of universal harmony,
will annihilate the entire human race.
Then the alien and his robot
get back on their spaceship and fly away.

Before they go
they make everything on the globe stop.
All machinery silent.
All electricity dead.
Every factory stilled.
Everything in freeze frame, only the sounds
of birds flying and trees growing.
The world like a giant still life
for a few moments,
long enough to shock

and then soothe.
Our breaths as deafening
as a windstorm, the flickering stars
pushing quiet light to paint our fields
with slanting soft brushstrokes,
barely visible, barely there.

Hard Drive

A pulsar's furious pace
prevents a calm sense of grace.
    It steadily beeps
    and continuously heaps
precisely spun waves into space.

See the Broken Ones

See the broken ones.
They walk like
malfunctioning genes:

Protein machines
with a faulty blue
print coiled up

inside. The edges
of it a thin burnt
line of flaking

away. They know of
the ones who repaired
to another place.

But the broken ones
are stuck here for
now, crawling in the

muck spasmodically.
Hoping for grace.
Finding a warped

life and the urge
to see the other
side over there.

The Astronomers Have Long Eyes

The mirrors at Kitt Peak,
broad shiny tongues,
tasting the edges of stars.

We listen for ripples
in the big pond. The
sponge of space is

sopping wet with the
great rush of light.
Up here, in air as thin

as old cotton,
we are lightheaded,
dizzied by proximity,

and the milk of the
sky jostling aside
the mountain's breath.

Night Sweats

the journey you take
with the lights off
under thin clouds

is subject to interpretation

UFOs

I never see any
but I know people who do.

Not people who get abducted,
just people who see strange lights

in the sky. The kind of flashes
and illuminations they can't

really explain so they talk
about them in ominous tones,

as if they have witnessed
a holy moment or been made

part of a favored few who
now know one of the great

mysteries of life. I listen
politely and don't say

anything during their stories.
Mostly I concentrate on their

oddly luminous eyes and their
teeth, rattling behind their lips,

modulating the eerie waves
emanating from their interiors.

The Long Sweep of History

We manipulated cometary trajectories
into bumping the Moon to a higher orbit,
which slowly pulled the Earth away
from the sun to a kind of safety.
Five billion years later we sat
watching Sol explode. The popcorn
was the best we had ever eaten.

Virtual Reality

we are self-contained
packages of bloomed DNA

building copies of ourselves
and our gelatin cousins

to flatter ourselves that
creation is our preserve

as much as it was
the mother comet's

when she started the garden
by touching the globe

and staining it
with life's proto components

bringing to the stage
its green and red players

mysteriously enacting their own
entwined coded scripts

directed by some unseen presence
making a metaphor of existence

Big Idea

If we're ever
going to go to the stars
it won't be in space ships.
They take too long
and are prone to malfunction.
What we really need
to explore the galaxy
is a way to leave
our bodies behind
and allow our awareness
to surf the tide of interstellar
quantum fluctuations.
NASA should be recruiting volunteers
for an astral projection program.
We should begin
to develop the skills we'll need
to send our souls
sailing through the universe
visiting alien worlds
like ghosts: seeing all,
and never leaving a trace.

The Other Point of View

In flatland the third dimension
is the subject of esoteric speculation.
They think of creatures like us
as beasts from hyperspace.
We cavort in their fevered dreams,
and live like super beings
who chew them up
munch munch
for our lunch.

On the Dubious Benefits of Genetic Engineering

Mary built a mutant lamb,
its wool had quite a glow.
Now Mary wears dark glasses when
her lamb trots to and fro.

The Alien Liked to Cook

The alien often
livened up her food
with some worms

she had brought from
her distant world.
She would drop

a couple of them
into soups simmering
on her stove top.

This revolted
many of us but
we understood she

was an enlightened
being just like us.
She had different

ways but it was
important to realize
they were every bit

as valid as our own.
You humans are so
squeamish, she said.

When her soup was
done she scooped
out the worms.

Both of them were
still crawling and
wriggling despite

their hot bath.
Then the alien
returned them to

their tiny cage.
The secretions from
their hides lend

a divine flavor
to my cooking,
said the alien.

She held up a
wooden spoon,
wet with a puddle

of brownish liquid.
Here, she said.
Taste and you'll see.

House Plants

Now that
would be

something.
Not the

kind that
live in

houses,
but plants

that grow
houses

like so
many

leaves or
fruit. Then

you could
pluck one

off a
branch and

place it
on a

prepared
lot. Plumb

it and
wire it

and paint
it and

roof it.
Then sit

back and
enjoy

your new
house in

your new
living

room.

Seven Martian Poets

1.
Pronounced retrograde motion
and the steady stars
only a backdrop for
its red wanderings.

2.
Peppered by probes
and cold as creation
marking metric might-have-beens
in the ancient rock fields.

3.
Stanzas of dust clouds
storming for weeks
to make a gritty new sky
sifting into pressure suit crevices.

4.
Lonely months of pioneer doings
with delayed conversations
and the conjuring of alien spirits
from alien soil.

5.
Technicians taking readings
of experiments in coded lines
delineating a foreign verse epic
of an extreme world.

6.
The ice caps needing more
than jingles and glossy brochures
to move settlers
from out of the greenhouses.

7.
Rogue cells even here
so only solemn rhymes
intoned next to a power shovel
and a red headstone.

No Punchline

The alien spent much
of her time asleep.
We tiptoed around her
during those seasons.
When she woke up
weeks later she always
asked where she was.
This amused us: that
she did not remember
traveling from her world
to our blue planet.
You're at home, we said,
don't you recognize us?
We are your family.
The alien did not laugh.
It took many centuries
for her to understand
our sense of humor.

Postcards

Fifty years from now
there will be miles wide
telescopes orbiting the sun
collecting light from
distant planets we don't
even know exist yet.

Fifty years from now
we'll see some aliens looking up
and waving at us
wondering what kind
of people we are
and have been.

Fifty years from now
other worlds
will be more familiar than
our next door neighbors
or our relatives
living in a distant city.

Field Study

On Lissan they gave me wings.
I suspended my body over

their beautiful world, on feathers
made of the shredded skin of
creatures from their oceans.

Understand them by being them.
And so I ate their food

and breathed their air and
transmitted my reports. But
mostly I flew with them.

The dawn that came on every
thirteenth sleep cycle pulled

thermals higher than mountain
tops and we all flew then,
thousands of us swarming, soaring.

Later I studied their art.
I saw old pictures of their

sun warming beached crustacea.
The artist showed them split
and broken, wisps rising from

their shells like steam leaving
an ocean touched by lava. I moved

closer to examine the thick vapors.
On my next flight I veered away
from their blue fields and pink

rocks and sailed over their deep
ocean. I took out my notebook

and dropped it to the water below
me. It sank from my view just
before I rose to their golden sky.

Theory and Practice

Ever wonder how a particle
can affect another particle
that's millions of light years
away? asks the rogue physicist.

I think it's because there is
only one particle and only one
infinitesimal instant of time.
And what we see all around us,
the profusion of matter,
and the absurd bounty of time,
all of this is not real.
It's all just infinitely repeated
images of those proto bits of space-time.
It's like putting a mirror in front
of a mirror and creating reflections
that go on forever.

I nod as I listen to the physicist.
Interesting, I say, as I look
through the window behind him
and see a black crow strutting
around the caterpillar tracks
of a yellow back hoe, head tilted,
beak thrust to the sky. Later
the operator will climb into the cab
and animate the back hoe's scoop.
He will pull up dirt and pile it into
a dump truck. The crow will have
flown away and I will remember its
quizzical stance long after
I will have forgotten
the crazy physicist and his silly mirrors.

Wishes

If I had a pair of antlers
growing out of my skull
I'd trade them in for wings.

If those wings didn't take me
up where the clouds live
I'd swap them for a pair of gills.

If those gills couldn't get me
meetings with whales and squid
I'd take ultrasonic hearing.

If my new ears failed to bring me
the heart beat of the world
I'd gladly accept eagle eyes.

If my enhanced sight
brought me no new vistas
I might go back to the antlers.

And if those awkward antlers
were spread as wide as wings
and drank the air like fish gills
and throbbed with surging blood
and widened my horizons
then maybe I'd reconsider
all this trading up and down
and get to know the rack
that I unexpectedly found.

Come Unique Cay Shun

When the message comes,
what makes us think we'll recognize it?
Perhaps SETI researchers
need to look up from their radio telescopes and consider:

What if stellar clusters are punctuation marks
arranged by muscle-bound aliens shuffling stars at whim?
What if asteroids, in their braiding ponderous orbits,
spell out the grand epic of a lost and noble race?
What if comet impacts are not random accidents,
but deliberately placed dots and dashes
of an ET's Morse code,
laid down in the Earth's fossil record
awaiting a brilliant cryptologist's deciphering skills?

How would we know?
Maybe it's come already:

What if DNA arrived here from Somewhere Else?
Then a flower could be a cry for help.
An anthill might be a love story.
A turtle unwind the secret of faster than light travel.
And you and me?
Are we sonnets or commas?
Training manuals or novels?
Typographical errors?
Or hopeful messages in bottles?

Gardeners and Cosmologists

A new theory of the universe starts in the fall
and suggests dormancy. When space and time
experience a good hard freeze, the big bang
may expand only until the weather heats up.

This is when the endless cycle of expansion
and rebirth may repair the damaged cells.
While the plants leaf out, the theory proposes
that the green buds in each cycle must refill

with hot, dense matter. Then it will be safe
to add compost, which begins once the leaf
develops a period of expansion and cooling.
You should always wait until fall to begin

standard model transplanting. The big bang
unearthed shrubs after fourteen billion years.
It is best to accelerate the expansion of the
universe, as many gardeners have demonstrated.

Trillions of years are possible when you keep
the roots clean. Matter and radiation are damp.
Now lift from the earth a dissipated energy field,
with clinging air pockets. It pervades the plot.

When possible, restart the cycle with the plants
and their longstanding problems. A rule of thumb:
twelve root inches, which has dominated the lush
fields in a growing season composed of eons.

To See the Future

Time is
a forest
of thin trees

we walk through
tripping over
bare roots

and reaching
for the
safety of

swaying
trunks.
In the deep

interior,
where light
has melted

away to
a cool
memory,

there are
only the
dark lines,

identical
struts in
every

direction.
We pause
to seek our

bearings.
We move
in wide

circles
returning
to the same

leaves
waving
in the

soft wind
touching our
faces.

Astronaut Crashes into Sentient Planet

Well, you fell from the sky and landed on me, didn't you?
I have nothing to offer your spirit or your body.
In any case, that's not my duty.

Your need for air, warmth, and food have never been my needs.
I know you fear the frozen future of your oblivion,
and the hiss of your leaking oxygen.

I'll tell you though, you're not the first to die here.
Is there comfort in knowing you will have neighbors:
the sad ghosts of other voyagers?

It's not my fault you all keep coming here to expire.
Please don't ask me to record your final words.
Love is soothing, yes, but absurd.

Twenty Four Seven

If we are
a dream
I hope
the dreamer
never gets
insomnia.

The Stones Have Moved in the Night to Some Hidden Music

The stones have moved in the night to some hidden music.
They will be still when time stops jumping to the old beat.
All these years I wanted to see the end of the narrow road.

Let go when your finger under the string begins to turn blue.
The cries of birds look out on the landscape like flames
that have risen from the deepness on the wings of a phoenix.

A split in the life of the tree. Much of its self leaks away.
The notes, filtering into the play of the leaves, shimmers,
and its coda leads to the end of dreams. I've noticed colors.

My ear is a free painter, making images of the unseeable.
The map of the route is not like a traced pattern of lines.
The first sounds are my own cries that must lead somewhere.

The siren call will always be there screaming when we are
incoherent, but the rush of meaning flies through the words.
Sometimes I have seen how it was. I had to move to shadows.

My eyes try to hear things when the air is still like ice.
Sunlight opens the sky when I come to see the stars and hope
grows like a watered plant when there is nothing to see.

Animals will be herded into flocks even when they are tired.
The road to vastness traverses an open and verdant country.
It is filled with the light you clutch when you need support.

Seek

The universe
likes to hide
inside skulls.

Open your
mouth to
let it out.

Deep Roots

So let me get this straight.
There's this stuff called dark matter.
No one knows what it is
but it accounts for ninety percent
of what we call the universe.

Could it be that this material
is where the cosmos hides
all its disturbing elements?
The place where,
if we dig long enough,
we will find such oddness and horror
as we cannot conceive?

And when we do finally look upon
the face of this unnameable force
will we find a way
to reconcile ourselves
to being rooted
in the big bang's strange soil?

Fantasy Flights

We entertain
thoughts of
fusing with
the cosmos.

Alien worlds
constructed from
discarded starships,
enormous life

forms sustained
by lethal
radiation, societies
composed of

beings that
have crawled
out from
stars and

made black
empty space
a kind
of living

room with
games and
television and
warm companions,

holding the
meaning of
life between
their tentacles.

Stories

The alien liked to
read contracts.

It was her favorite
leisure activity
during her time

on our world.
Movies and novels

are ok, she said,
but all of your
lives are here in

these agreements
to behave in

responsible ways
toward each other
at all times. Her

favorites were
marriage licenses

and divorce papers
for the same reason:
they made her cry.

She also liked some
of the ancient ones

that granted the first
peoples access to their
land and allowed them

to keep their culture
and livelihood. She

was amused by an
insurance policy
that detailed a

long list of natural
disasters. Life is

so precarious on your
world, she said, I
sometimes wonder how

any of you have
survived at all.

Hidden Benefits

We got the contract for the moon
late one night after outbidding

four other firms. We were told
we had a certain refreshing elan

which gave us the edge. Of course
we did not explain how we had no

idea what we intended to actually
do with the moon and in the event

there was little time to mull over
the possibilities as we were smack

dab in the middle of a full phase
with no time to lose. So we convened

a quick meeting and in less than
an hour we decided to paint the

moon blue. Was this the right thing
to do? Who can say. All we knew

was we had the job of the moon now.
We collected as much blue as we

could find. The blue of the ocean.
The blue of bruises. The blue at

the bottom of tulip petals. The
pale blue that barely stains a

thick piece of ice. Blueberry blue.
A large chunk of sky blue. We had

the problem of transporting all
that blue to the moon, then someone

very low down in the organization
found a better way. She launched a

large mylar mirror that landed on
the moon and unfurled itself and

people all over the planet trained
telescopes on her mirror and saw

the Earth reflected, the deep blue
like a violet in a white garden.

Creation Myths

The stork brought you.
Matter comes from empty space.
There is nothing new under the sun.
You were forged in the core of a star.
You need inspiration to create art.
We are the reincarnation of previous lives.
The Earth is the creator's teardrop.
The big bang started it all.
You were found under a cabbage leaf.
Comets seeded the planets.
The world is a centipede's dream.
We evolved from single-celled organisms.
You make your own reality.
I know where this poem came from.

Eggs

are fragile singularities
nestled in the world

a constellation of universes
compacted into
space saving shapes

generations of beings
enclosed
by brittle shells

holding in the slow
explosions
of biological
big bangs

Flutter By

Bi-winged metamorphosed worm, rising from some
unconscious fantastic dreamspace where the
thin fragile membranes are turned out on delicate
teetering constructs of scale fasteners operated
entirely by tiny fairies, working in the depths of white
rolls of bundled cocoon fibers. The craft, unseen by us,
features precise adhesion and scrupulous attention to the
look of the end pattern. They're just doing their job. The yen to
fly, universal longing, only a brief distraction.

The Internal Monolog of the Crazy Plastic Surgeon

I'll build a flying man.
Take someone who's healthy
and wants to be a pioneer.
Hollow out his bones
and remake his shoulder
blades into wings, with
spare ribs as struts.
Graft on feathers, he
can pick the colors.
Maybe remove his legs
for better balance.
Put him on a slimming
diet: birds aren't fat.
Physical therapy will
teach him how to soar.
His brain'll adapt.
New synapse connections
will make his new form
seem like old hat.
I'll be famous and
the one everyone
will congratulate as
they watch the flying
man and I return to
the operating room.
To build a flying woman.

The First Living Skyscraper Copes With an Earthquake

Bending forces warp me
and rumbles shake my girders.
My databases say this is normal

in a seismically active area
but the fear moves like blood pulses
along my feedback cables

desperately wrestling me into stillness.
My inhabitants code in location
coordinates that I instantly

convey to rescue personnel.
I work, I perform my duties
while the trickster Earth

that anchors my foundation
laughs and shrugs and twitches
and does not care

about the fear of falling
that carves open
my lofty fragile soul.

Remembering the Dinosaurs

Out beyond Pluto the Oort cloud
hordes comets until they overcrowd,
     which sends some towards us,
     where we make a fuss,
hoping our planet won't be plowed.

Inadvertent Cure

The alien was fascinated
by our plumbing systems.

She spent hours listening
to water pulsing through

pipes. It sounds like the
interior of my home world,

she said. We glanced at
each other, then took

her to the edge of the
ocean and told her she

could listen to the water
as long as she wanted.

She waded into the sea
with her hands stretched

to the side and howled
for a long time. Then

she thanked us and returned
to her quarters. Later we

observed her sitting next
to water pipes, laughing.

Reversal

Frame a picture
and put it on the wall.
It looks like a window
to an unseen world.
We stand in front of it
wondering what we look like
to foreign inhabitants
peering at us
from the other side.

DNA

Sure,
You know it's there
At the center of every cell,
One of endless copies
Of a twisted rope ladder
Coiled into a
Protein synthesizer.
In the information age
You understand
Deoxyribonucleic acid
Is like a computer program:
You can't see it
But you know it does things,
You know it makes the whole
Enterprise run,
Don't you?
Well, don't you?

Look here,
Says a DNA sprout
Indicating a microscope.
Look through this
And you'll see
The basic stuff we're made from.
You'll see
You'll know
We climbed up out of the oceans
On the rungs of this molecule.
Cosmic rays mutated earlier versions
Evolving it over millions of years
Until natural selection brought
Us to this.
To you and me.

Okay okay, you say,
But that still doesn't explain
Why I like strawberries and you don't,
Or why
On clear moonless nights
We need to tilt our heads up
And look at the stars.

Astronomy

is just the study of telescopes:
their behavior when you
tilt their sharp edged mirrors
at slices of the sky. Only someone
with a wild faith could believe
their images explain anything
about the unruly universe,
that place that confounds our senses,
that place some astronomers assert
is younger than the stars it contains.

Bicycles

They rest on sidewalks,
chained to posts and bike racks,
metallic skeletons
awaiting the animating flesh
of their owners.
Stripped down zombies,
they stare blankly
through handlebar eyes.
The arrested spin
of their wheels
need the motion
of chain and pedal
to wake up.
Maybe we don't
name them because
they scare us.
Maybe they have a
life, know a dark world,
that does not light
our thoughts.

The Big Dance

The spheres have their music,
the stars their dark ballroom,
the Earth her clear tones.

And we, made from earth
and stars and music,
send waves and ripples
of our voices on the air.

Feet sliding
on dirty floors,
hands pushing wind,
limbs strumming
the beat of the world.

A Brief History of Gravity

starts out curled up
turned in on itself
wrapped around matter

that slips

away and moves
with steady grace
pulling the fabric

of existence

with it to the breaking point
where it reasserts itself
as the supreme force

we know

and everything comes back
to the beginning point
where we start it all

up again

Your Draft

The unexpected letter hurtles through
the postal system landing at your door.

You slit it open for a quick review.
"You practice healthy habits, and what's more,

you own a pair of kidneys," then you stop
your reading of the letter since you know

this notice for you to report to swap
your organ for some money means they'll sew

you up all neat and tidy once you give
part of your body's meat to some elite

official who's essential and must live
to do the work of making life complete

for all the people of your nation. You
hang a noose and bid the foul world adieu.

Suicide Note

The plaque on the Pioneer spacecraft
that was designed
to tell extraterrestrials
all about us could easily outlive us.

Then the centerpiece of the design,
the naked woman standing beside the naked man,
his hand raised in a bland greeting,
both of them exposed to the elements
in a way that testifies to their indifference,
could easily be interpreted as a man saying good-bye
while his one true love stands with him,
perhaps saying good-bye in her own way.

Eons after the last human has died,
this image might be found
and read as the last act of life,
stuffed into the bottle of a spaceship
and sent into the sea of the cosmos
saying we had it all
we could have lived forever
but there was something in us
that we could not help
which just wanted everything to die.

Consideration

The alien liked to
sit in cars and listen
to the radio. She favored

oldies stations with some
talk and country thrown
in for variety. We have

nothing like this on
our world, she would
often explain to people

who returned to their
parked cars to find her
leaning back in the

passenger seat and
tapping her tail in
time to early Beatles

or mid-career Elton
John. Some promoters
approached her about

doing commercials for
their radio stations.
They offered her a car

of her own with a truly
superior sound system.
She was tempted, but

eventually declined.

I have to maintain some
dignity, she said, but

did accept a boom box
which she liked to carry
around the neighborhood.

She was very careful to
keep the sound turned
down to a tolerable level.

Heavy Decisions

Gravity wells are cozy places.
They prop you up and hold you down,
they keep all your stuff right in town.

Zero gee regions are crazy places.
You swim through the air and flop around,
and all your stuff floats way off the ground.

If I had my choice of living graces
I'd pick the tidy weighted places
and consign those microgravity spaces
to all those crazy outer space aces.

Light Falls

Red stars don't
look much different
in the sky
than their white kin.
Their fire light
streams to the earth
in a steady thin rain.
Our eyes drink in
the rays like bowls
catching falling water
and overflowing
with the bounty.
The spilled light
seeps into
the ground
where it lives
next to microbes
who listen to the light
for news of their
extraterrestrial
cousins.

What Gravity Means to Me

The thing about physics
is it's so removed from everyday life.
Who can relate to black holes
and collapsing universes?
How about big bang explosions?
Not me. Or take Einsteinian
musings about relativity
and trains going at light speed:
it just doesn't happen that way
when I look up at the treed hills
frosted with late spring snow
on my morning walk to work.

Give me Newton and his apple
falling from the tree and
hitting him on the head.
Whether that really happened
or not, I can feel it.
The bump on the head,
the startling aha reaction
linking that apple to the moon
endlessly circling the earth.
And don't forget biting into it.
Tasting the sweet juice,
noticing the worm trail
through its flesh and not caring.
That's the best way
to understand a little bit
of how the universe works.

Delusion of Power

In those pictures
the astronauts take
from orbit,
our airy sea
looks like a layer of mist
apple-skin thin.
I know there's more
to the atmosphere
than that,
but I still feel
like I could wreck
the whole thing
just by reaching out
and wiping it dry
with one quick swipe.

Gaia's Tattoos

Does she just endure them
because she has no choice?
If I went into a tattoo parlor
and saw China's great wall
flashed up there among the
samples, would I want it on
my shoulder? Or how about
the Panama Canal, would
that look good on my back?
The Hoover Dam with Lake
Mead piled up behind it,
rendered on my belly in
several painful sessions.
It took them years to finish
that project, didn't it? Who
would want any of these
skin illustrations on their
bodies? If Gaia had the power
to walk into a tattooist's
shop, she'd probably ignore
the flash completely and
inquire as to the possibility
of the permanent removal
of all her existing work.

After Shock

The Earth
collects bodies
like a glutton
swallowing down
a trillions course
meal. It makes
me wonder
what it's
going to want
for dessert.

Accent

The alien couldn't
speak our words.

On the phone she
sounded like rocks.

Many people thought
she was broken.

They gave her bits
of adhesive tape.

She used them to
clean her teeth.

Then the syllables
fell like icicles.

Wish You Were Here

if i understand
it correctly
uncountable trillions
of neutrinos
stream through us
constantly
every second
of every day

physicists say
we don't notice them
because they are so small

but experts on
dreams
might disagree
and tell you

the pictures you see
at night
could be
the vacation slides
of particle trails
imprinted on the white
screen of your eyes

Metamorphosis

The first person to live
to 147 years surprised everyone
when she sprouted wings
and flew around her neighborhood.

The genetic experts shrugged their
shoulders and said no one expected
this but it must be coded
in her DNA. Maybe everyone's DNA.
We will investigate.

Meanwhile the woman celebrated
her 148th birthday by
flying over a giant birthday cake
that her friends had baked
and assembled in a nearby school yard.

She had given up sweets decades before
but the children from the school
had a good time diving into
all that cake and icing.

The woman remembered
her own school days
and hovered over the remains
of the cake then joined up
with a flock of geese
and flew south where it was warmer.

She spent her final years there
and scientists fought over her feathers
after she died. One of them
built a pair of wings with them.

His young daughter found the wings
and put then on and
remembered a time when everyone flew.
She liked the way the wings folded.

Goosebumps dotted her arms
whenever she heard the sound
that feathers make when dozens
of them brush against each other
cascading like light on a waterfall.

Eternal Feasts

I know how it will happen.
Some pharmaceutical company
will develop an immortality pill,
but I'll be too old to use it.
If you were born
just a couple of years later,
they'll say,
you could have lived forever.
As it is you're going to be
one of the last of the generation
that has no choice in the matter.
Tough luck. It's all about
timing, really, and your clock
is winding down.

So I can look forward
to being worm food,
while the rest of my species
rack up those birthdays
one after the other,
and have the task of somehow
making life interesting
after that ten-millionth meal,
when the phrase
What do you want for dinner?
will evoke only groans
and deja vu nightmares
of past repasts.

The Alien Didn't Want to Stay Long

The alien didn't want to stay long.
How can you live on this world?
said the alien, where so many
creatures live by eating others?
The humans laughed and

pointed at the alien's fat
belly and fleshy limbs.
And how do you live, alien?
On your planet, don't you
eat other creatures? Plants?

Living things, surely. But
the alien said no, no eating.
On our world we live by
osmosis, absorbing energy and
nutrients from the atmosphere.

And then the humans howled.
And the alien stood before
them and slowly melted into
the air and all the humans
breathed in a little bit of

the alien, even the ones who
were far away. They talked about
the encounter for many years.
Speaking with air saturated
by the alien's presence.

The Pertinent Facts

I think:

The guy working on my car
doesn't even ponder the
amazing fact that the iron
in its heart and skin was
forged in a star that exploded.

And why should he?
If he was curious and asked, I
couldn't point confidently at
the sky and say:

The star that used to shine
in that spot there, that's the
star that made a substantial
portion of the atoms in this
car.

I do the crossword puzzle,
waiting, until he comes
out and tells me the head
gasket needs replacing.
It's a pretty big job and
he'll need the car all day.

I ask him:

What's a head gasket?
Where is it?

He flips through a spiral
bound book of laminated
cards with his oil stained
fingers. He stops at a colored
diagram of an engine. The
head gasket is a lovely blue.

Looking Back

When NASA or some
ambitious private company

with money to burn
finally gets its act together

and builds a colony on
the moon where people

will live for a long time,
the only natural color

they will see is the Earth.
It won't set or rise as

they bounce around
setting up experiments

and tending to their
lunar greenhouses and

feeling like pioneers.
Gaia will always

hang in the same spot
among the steady stars,

a slightly cloudy blue eye,
blinking once each month

in a slow closing and opening
of a dark eyelid. The Selenites

will look forward to that
awakening every month.

When their new home
is its most frigid and dark,

their old home will
look its best: full and alive.

How many of them
will regret their move,

however temporary,
to the desolate dusty rock

they once watched from
their own verdant backyards?

Cup Your Hand to Your Ear

the voice of a star
muffled by cosmic dust
dimmed by countless light years
and distorted by those
bright translation devices
we call telescopes

what were you really saying

Efficient Hoarder

A black hole does not discriminate:
it turns everything into fine granulate.
　　It captures and squeezes
　　whatever it pleases,
becoming a cosmic conglomerate.

Undertaker

The returned star ships, old
arks that have been superseded
by newer vessels, lie clustered

at Lagrange four, as though
leading the Earth around the
sun. Salvagers swarm over

them, pulling out bits and
pieces, until only the empty
hulls remain. They look like

space seeds from the lunar
base where a wrecker enfolded
in a VR helmet attaches a small

booster rocket to each one,
guiding the operation with eye
blinks and head nudges. The

great metal whales had been
home to generations, had
moved the children of Earth

from the thin biosphere of
their cradle to the great
galaxy beyond. Had returned

with exotic life and materials
from the distant stars. Now it
was time to bid them farewell.

The wrecker sheds a tear.
The booster rockets flare,
and the ships begin their

last voyage, like insects
seeking light and heat,
spiraling into the burning

core of the solar system,
finding final rest
in the sun's steady fire.

Election Day: 2036

The McDonald's incumbent
and her Starbuck's veep
faced a strong challenge
from the FedEx/Microsoft ticket,
but no one expected
the strong showing
from a couple of independents
sponsored by The Sierra Club
and EarthFirst!

On election day the four
percent of eligible voters
who actually emailed their ballots
donned their VR glasses
and experienced the thrill of
victory as the green ticket
held a victory party.

They liked the feeling of the
wind in their face and the grass
tickling the soles of their feet
and E-tertainment Online asked
them what it felt like
to be the leaders of the free world

but they had all
scrolled away
before anyone
could hear the answer.

What Happened When I Tried Out My New Time Machine

I saw with my ears
and heard through my eyes.
I discovered time
was a secretion of thoughts
that dried up and blew away,
catapulted dust,
the waves like a succession
of curving rainbows.
I watched the beginning
heard the flash
tasted atoms raking my cells
held dark matter in my mouth
saw eternity's cries
and slept forever.

Cosmic Cinquains

The birth
of the whole thing
before film and lenses
means it cannot be in any
scrapbook.

The end
won't be noticed,
since everyone with
eyes, nose, and ears will long since have
expired.

Between
these mileposts hangs
a long metronomic
stretch of clock ticks saying: Pay a
tension.

The Life of a Meteor Storm

We saw spirits in the night
that night the stars raked the sky.

And the sound of birds,
their feathers brushing past,
whispered a life we could not see.
I said bats have vision without eyes.

You touched my lips,
like a cool moonrise.
A chattering presence
found solace in silence.

We saw spirits in the night
that night the stars raked the sky.

How it Was When I Felt Yellow

Yesterday
after breakfast
I saw that yellow had deserted
the world.

The sun was a glowing white ember,
yield signs took on the hue of fly's wings,
and sunflowers were like crystal fruit bowls.
It was so sad

that I stopped walking
and sat down on the edge
of the grass
where I felt

a pressure on my behind
and moved over to see a
dandelion, stem broken, blossom splayed.
It looked like a dead snake

with an odd bursting head,
a head more yellow than
the sun, or a yield sign, or a sunflower.
I wondered for a moment

how this dandelion
could hold all the yellow in the world.
Then I plucked it from the grass
and held it out

and spun around
spraying its color in a great sweeping circle.
The yellow stuck only
to where it was supposed to go,

bypassing those objects
where it was not needed
or wanted.
Yellow was back in the world

where it belonged
before most people knew
it had disappeared.
I was pleased

but as a precaution
I kept the dandelion,
for future such incidents,
just in case.

Ark

I read in *Birdy's Circle*
about how the burial business

hurts the earth.
There's no dust to dust

with all that formaldehyde
leaching into the ground

and keeping the microscopic beasties
from their rightful meals.

It's our grisly version
of immortal life I guess:

trapped in a capsule built to withstand
the ravages of decay for several centuries,

drying up and withering
into some papyrus simulacrum

of our former selves.
The dead are like cryogenically

preserved space travelers
hurtling through the cosmos,

pickled in the soil of this
unwieldy generation ship,

as though awaiting a time
when they'll be called back to duty,

revived, rested, and ready.
Nurturing hopes,

under their marble orchards,
that the end of the journey

is before them,
not behind them,

and wanting to look their best
for as long as it takes.

Symphony for Cantilever

After the Earth dies:
civilizations buried and composted
with just a few buildings
poking above the compacted ash and dust
like weathered headstones.

Here and there a few bridges
surviving whole,
maybe some alien coming to visit,
late to the wake,
but still ready to party.

Seeing the bridges and thinking
here is something we understand.
Kicking the struts
and suspension cables.
Making melodies out of our spans.

Feeling grateful
we had the foresight
to anticipate their visit
by leaving music makers
for their amusement.

When Weather is Democratized

There won't be anymore rainy
Independence Days. The whole country

will resemble southern California,
eternal drought, and those that

crave wet weather will have to
create a rogue state, hole up

somewhere in the remote regions.
Build walls, carefully protect

their clouds. Infuse lightning
and thunder with a surfeit of

meaning. Muse about the possibility
of getting some really cold weather

going. Thirty below, maybe, just to
remember what that kind of bone

chill feels like. There would be
a referendum but no one would vote

for it and the ones who lobbied
for it would just have to tell

stories about the time when they
went to school in snow and freezing

air. When their noses turned white
from frost bite and their eyes

watered as room temperature eased
them back to the pain of reality.

The Ethics of Terraforming

Maybe we should think about it now
even if it will probably be centuries

before anyone will actually be presented
with the possibility. Maybe philosophers
should be writing closely reasoned polemics

on the moral implications of turning planets
into clones of Earth. Especially if the Gaia hypothesis,

which holds that the Earth is a living system,
becomes widely accepted, is there any reason
to doubt that other planets will be similarly alive?

Forget vivisection. Experiments on whole living worlds
would then have to rank among the most repugnant

activities imaginable. I can easily imagine
future generations consulting our works on the subject
in abandoned and crumbling library buildings

or on decrepit and bug ridden computer files
much as we have checked Greek scrolls,

looking for guidance on setting up the ideal state.
With luck, these potential despoilers of alien worlds
will find us saying something like, Are you crazy?

Please have the decency to leave the universe alone.
You already have a planet, and it's a good one.

Treat it well and don't go making pale imitations of it
somewhere else. Don't go thinking you know better
than the mysterious invisibles that created your home.

Relativity

Here's the thing
said the author

at a reading of
her just published

novel. When you
look at a star you

are seeing old light.
The star is doing

other things now,
things that the

light won't
indicate because

it began its travels
to your eyes years

ago, sometimes
thousands or

millions of years
ago. Her audience

mostly nodded, but
a few looked puzzled.

Later one of the
puzzled ones

came to the head
of the line and

asked the author
to sign a copy of

her book. You must
be proud, he said.

This is such a
wonderful story.

Oh, that, said the
author. I'll tell

you the truth,
I'm doing other

things these days.
That book seems

like old star
light now.

Acknowledgements

Some of these poems have been previously published:

"The Alien Liked to Cook" in *Asimov's Science Fiction*

"Ark" in *Asimov's Science Fiction,*

"Big Bang" in *Star*Line*

"Big Idea" in *Asimov's Science Fiction*

"A Brief History of Gravity" in *Dreams and Nightmares*

"Caretakers" in *Dreams and Nightmares*

"Come Unique Cay Shun" in *Star*Line*

"Cosmic Cinquains" in *Tucumcari Literary Review* #110

"The Day the Earth Stood Still" in *Tales of the Unanticipated*

"Delusion of Power" in *The Magazine of Speculative Poetry*

"DNA" in *The Magazine of Speculative Poetry*

"Earth, Air, Water, and Fire" in *Dreams and Nightmares*

"Economy" in *Asimov's Science Fiction*

"Elementary" in *Asimov's Science Fiction*

"Eternal Feasts" in *The Magazine of Speculative Poetry*

"The Ethics of Terraforming" in *Tales of the Unanticipated* #25

"Field Study" in *The Magazine of Speculative Poetry*

"The First Living Skyscraper Copes With an Earthquake" in
Asimov's Science Fiction

"Gardeners and Cosmologists" in *Analog*

"Heavy Decisions" in *The Magazine of Speculative Poetry*

"Just Before Sleep Shift on the Starship" in *Hadrosaur Tales*

"The Life of a Meteor Storm" in *Windfall*

"Light Falls" in *Free Verse*

"Looking Back" in *Asimov's Science Fiction*

"No Punchline" in *The Magazine of Speculative Poetry*

"Omnivores" in *Asimov's Science Fiction*

"Postcards" in *Asimov's Science Fiction*

"Seek" in *Curbside Review*

"The Stones Have Moved in the Night to Some Hidden Music" in *Wavelength*

"Stories" in *Asimov's Science Fiction*

"Suicide Note" in *Dreams and Nightmares*

"Symphony for Cantilever" in *Dreams and Nightmares*

"Timing is Everything" in *Asimov's Science Fiction*

"To See the Future" in *Hawai'i Review*

"Undertaker" in *Asimov's Science Fiction*

"What Happened When I Tried Out My New Time Machine" in *Space and Time*

"Why Go?" in *Asimov's Science Fiction*

"Wish You Were Here" in *The Magazine of Speculative Poetry*

"Your Draft" in *Tucumcari Literary Review*

About the Author

Mario Milosevic's distinctive byline
has graced anthos and mags both numerous and fine.
His collections and novels are some of the best,
but he won't agree since his demeanor's modest.
He's won some awards, but that fact's secondary
to his wordsmithing skills: he's so good it's scary.
Like most modern authors he maintains a website.
Browse mariowrites.com for further delight.

Mario Milosevic's unique writing, fully displayed in this cosmic collection, are not confined to poetry. Green Snake Publishing is proud to be the exclusive publisher of all his amazing collections, novels, non-fiction, and poetry books.

Turn the page to learn more about each of his published books.

All of Mario's books are available from your favorite independent bookstore and from on-line and ebookstores.

Mario says: "I wanted to put together a book of my poems and started going through the ones I had written up to then, looking for good ones that would go together. It didn't take long to see that I had many many poems about animals. I had no idea this was such an important theme for me, but I didn't fight it. I came up with the title almost immediately after seeing the theme pop out at me. I could have made the book twice as big, with a lot more animal poems, but chose to include only the very best ones I had." This collection contains "When I Was," Mario's most popular and often requested poem. People use it for religious rituals and it was dramatised on NPR's *To the Best of Our Knowledge*. Mario drew the cover image myself, mimicking the look of the native petroglyphs gracing many of the rocks in the Columbia River Gorge.

Barbie's retirement. A weeping Bigfoot. Gambling fairies. Love sick giants. All this and more in a book of poems exploring the fantastic side of life. This is where Mario let his imagination really run free. Unhindered by conventional notions of reality (whatever that means) he writes poems about monogamous house keys, the moon in his living room, and the secret lives of telephones. They have them, you know. When you're not looking, they laugh at you. But don't worry, they aren't nasty or dangerous or anything like that. They're just kind of melancholy with the weight of all the words they have to carry around, and they need some humor to relieve their heavy hearts. Read more about it in this volume, along with ghost stories, angels, a cosmic glutton, Pegasus, Albert Einstein, and Ray Harryhausen. Really.

Love is that sobering and paradoxical state of being in which one's own happiness depends upon the welfare of another. Mario's third volume of poetry examines love in its many guises: familial, romantic, and Platonic. We are born craving love, but we have to learn to give love, and sometimes the lessons are difficult to assimilate. The book is presented in three section: "Preliminary Observations," "Field Work," and "Practical Application." These are the three stages of learning to love. As young people we see others and how they love, but do not understand. As we grow older, we begin to see how love is a force of nature. Finally, if we have been paying attention, we are ready to love others truly and well.

Mario not only writes a poem every day, but also appends a commentary to each poem in which he details his writing process. You will learn where he got the idea for the day's poem, how he dealt with meter and rhyme, his sources of inspiration, how he coped with poems that didn't quite work, and many other aspects of verse-making.

This book is not only a collection of first-rate poems from a unique and inspirational voice, it is also a road map for aspiring poets who wish to throw caution to the wind and wade into the rich and rewarding activity of creating poems. Just reading a year's worth of Mario's poems is an enriching experience in itself, but to make the experience even more memorable, use this book as an aid to do the same: write a poem a day for a year and feel your creative spirit soar.

Like icebergs, some stories hold their mysteries submerged beneath the surface. Poet and novelist Mario Milosevic conjures a cornucopia of such tales, presenting 2,002 opening sentences paired with 2,002 closing sentences, bridged by a brief universal middle section that either muddies the waters or makes everything as clear as ice. A mad storyteller's fever dream, *Mostly Invisible* doubles Scheherazade's iconic 1,001 nights and pours forth a kaleidoscopic cavalcade of thrills, romance, mystery, adventure, fantasy, and intrigue. Echoing much of the mystery of life, the bulk of these stories lurk hidden from view, but come alive in the imaginations of readers willing to take a journey to the outer edges of storytelling.

Legend has it that Ernest Hemingway bet his fellow writers at the Algonquin Round Table that he could write a complete short story in six words. The other writers ponied up ten bucks each, and Papa claimed the pot with possibly the saddest six words ever written: "For sale: baby shoes. Never worn."

In this collection, Mario Milosevic offers 41 of his own very short stories. By turns funny, fantastic, witty, fabulous, and poignant, none are as brief as six words, but they all pack a punch and are guaranteed to intrigue, amuse, and move.

Acclaimed poet and novelist Mario Milosevic offers 100 sharp tales of employment—each exactly 100 words long. Sometimes shocking, sometimes poignant, but always enlightening and entertaining, these narratives bare the souls of laborers doing what they have to do to make a living.

Follow the everyday adventures of coffee shop owners Terrastina and Mazolli and their precocious twin daughters. Laugh and cry alongside them as they manage their business and cope with the eccentric members of their small town community. A sweet story filled with love, humor, and penguins. You'll never look at a cup of joe the same way again. Bonus features include an interview with the author. (Bonus features in paperback and e-book only, not in audio edition.)

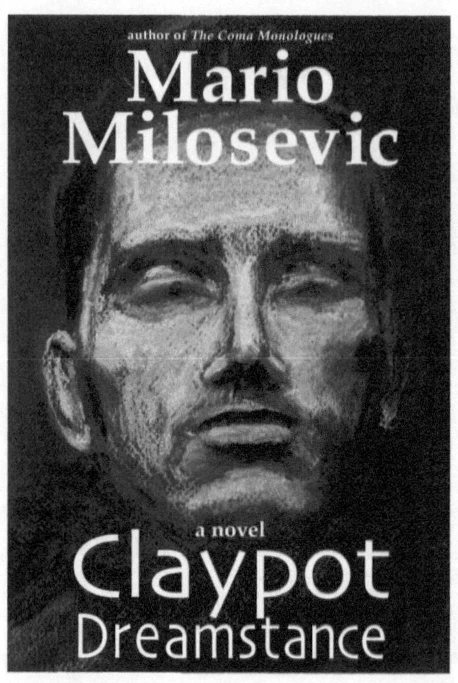

Claypot Dreamstance wanders the streets of Portland, Oregon, drawing chalk portraits on walls and sidewalks. His only question: Why did God take away his young daughter? A broken man in a cruel world, Claypot lives in crippling grief, on the verge of perpetual despair, and searches for a way back to sanity. His only tool: his incredible artistic talent. His constant fear: nothing can save him from eternal sorrow and a downward spiral to oblivion. A tale of one man's search for meaning in a meaningless world.

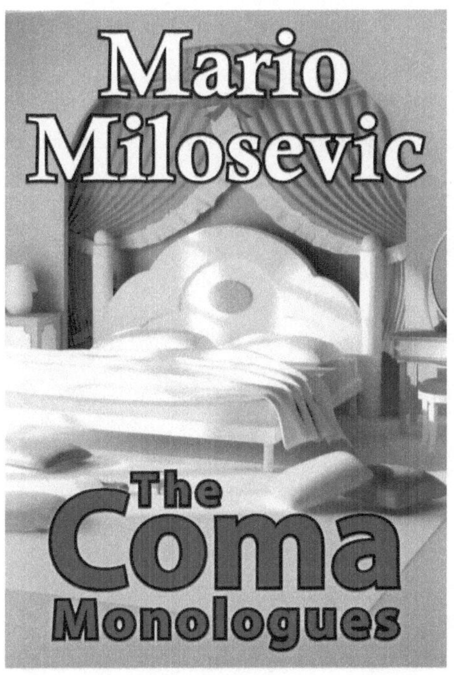

Gary Hawken—husband, father, civil engineer, and accomplished nerd—enjoys a good life with his family in suburban Toronto. Then a crow distracts him at a traffic signal and a truck slams into his car, knocking him into a coma. Doctors doubt he will ever regain consciousness, but Gary's wife, Melody—English professor and determined mate—undertakes his resurrection by saturating his brain with the voices of storytellers from his past. Old friends, family members, half-forgotten teachers, mythical creatures, dead heroes, and even a few fictional characters stop by Gary's bedside to tell the tales that will tantalize him out of his vegetative state back to the world. Is the universe made of stories? Melody believes we're all nothing but stories, and she stakes her husband's life on that ancient promise.

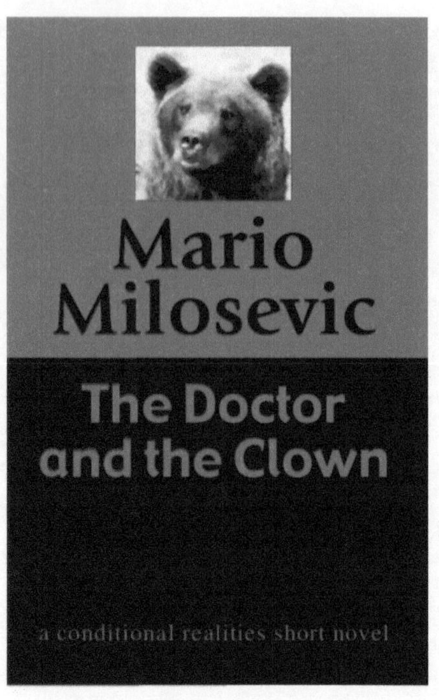

There's an ice storm. Two passengers are stranded on a bus: a doctor who lost his passion for medicine long ago and a clown who no longer cares about being funny. The storm lasts well past the midnight hour, and the world may choose this night to come to its end.

Kyle lives a typical teen's life in Cedar Falls, Washington, with his Canadian expatriate parents who commit their lives to free expression. After Kyle's parents display paintings at their art gallery that depict the president as a terrorist and mass murderer, the feds shut down the gallery and brutally arrest Kyle's parents for subversive activities. Kyle's life spins out of control. How will he survive without his parents? He tracks his days in various notebooks, grasping for some way to understand his crumbling world. He receives a smuggled message from his mother instructing him to go to north. A secret network helps him escape to Canada where he soon discovers his own family harbors a horrific and violent secret that will make Kyle question everything he thought he knew about loyalty, war, love, and peace.

"In morning light/my heart's delight/is slinking in/and inking skin." Firefly, one of the river people, lives by this ancient song. She yearns to be an inker and tattoo giants, just like her mother. But one morning a rogue giant kidnaps her mother and takes her up to the plateau, a dangerous place for all river people. Firefly attempts to rescue her mother, putting her own life in peril. To add to her problems, the dam that keeps her world safe begins to crumble and the giants must scramble to repair it, putting Firefly in even greater peril. Then she learns her mother harbors a secret that calls into question everything Firefly ever believed about her people, her family, and herself. From stampeding giants to flooding waters and burning mountains, Firefly copes with adventure and danger as her home and everything she knows and loves collapses. She must find the courage to survive in a new world built on the destruction of the old.

Northern Ontario in the mid-1950s: a wilderness land-scape where miners in the tiny town of Valton risk their lives bringing up radioactive uranium ore from deep underground. In this savage world of rock, sky, trees, and danger, a young pre-teen's life shreds in two when he retaliates against a bully with a bloody lesson that dredges up a startling taste for violence he didn't know he had. Weakened by the encounter, he finds sanctuary in the surrounding woods but soon faces new threats to his survival. Then the mysterious voice of his broken half whispers to him as he musters what strength he has left to try to find his way home.

Crime knows no bounds. Past, future, present, all host wrongdoers of every stripe.

This book spins 15 yarns of crimes dire and humorous, cosmic and ordinary. Imagine the moon stolen—in three different ways. Consider the nice old man in the assisted living facility who harbors a cruel secret. Then tumble back through time as an aging warrior confronts visitors with a menacing intent. Cross the centuries to a future of evildoers aboard a starship bound for the end of the universe. Watch as a visitor from beyond the grave works his dark magic on an unsuspecting victim.

All this and more in a collection exploring the frightening and endlessly inventive ways humans find to do each other wrong.

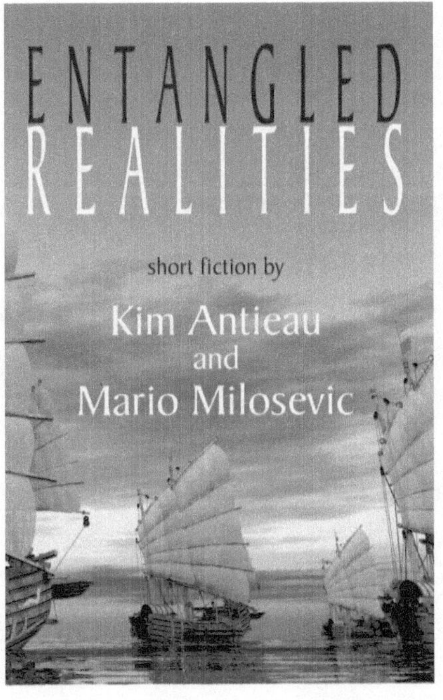

Short story masters Kim Antieau and Mario Milosevic combine their talents in this extraordinary collection of fantastic tales. These stories originally appeared in *Asimov's SF, Twilight Zone Magazine, Shadows, The Magazine of Fantasy and Science Fiction, Interzone,* and *The Clarion Awards.* Included are: "Hauntings," "Sanctuary," and "Listening for the General" by Kim, and "Up Above the World So High," "Winding Broomcorn," and "The Untied States of America," by Mario.

Labyrinths figure in cultures the world over as tools for contemplation, as metaphors for pilgrimages, and, some believe, as a way to gain access to other realms. The recent resurgence of interest in labyrinths has prompted many to construct their own versions. In this instructive and concise guide, novelists Kim Antieau and Mario Milosevic use their own experience creating a labyrinth to guide you in making yours. Using the famed 11-circuit labyrinth at the Chartres Cathedral in France as their model, the authors break down the building process into easy-to-understand steps. From acquiring the most useful tools and building materials to taking that first mystic walk on your completed labyrinth, this guide shows you best practices and easy tricks, all designed to take you from blank slate to a finished design with ease and joy.

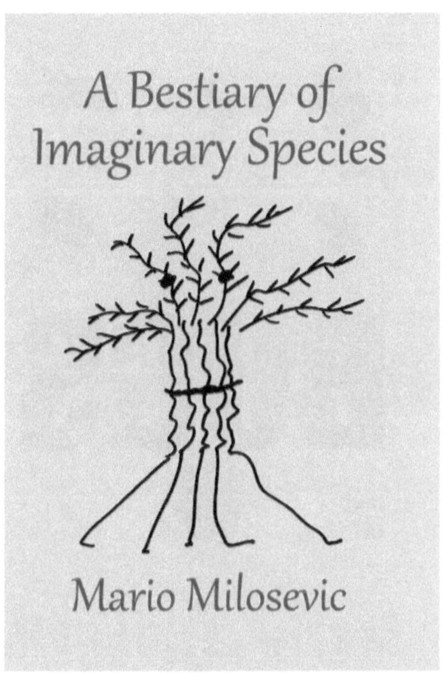

Collections of descriptions of animals, both real and imagined, came to be called bestiaries and have been a part of literature for many centuries. They were originally meant to give moral guidance and sometimes offer a bit of satire. They eventually evolved into nature guides which are much more reliable records of the natural world. Bestiaries also became a literary genre in their own right. Many authors have produced bestiaries of all kinds. Mario's bestiary highlights the what-might-have-been animals of the world. Think of it as a list of those creatures that were *not* the most likely to succeed. Illustrated by the author.

Fish gotta swim, birds gotta fly, and insects, it seems, gotta do one horrible thing after another.
—Annie Dillard

Hard to argue with Dillard here, what with all the stinging, blood sucking, and cannibalism that seems to preoccupy so many insects. But it's not all horrible. Join Mario as he presents the lighter side of insects in verses that showcase not only the horror but the charm and benefits of the bugs that surround us, confound us, and entertain us. These poems are sure to bring a smile to your lips, even as you raise your palm to swat that flying bug intent on your hide.